the Santa papers:
an unauthorized autobiography

by Wally Metts

Hope it's a
" good read"!

thanks,

Santa

For mom,
and for other believers

the Santa papers:
an unauthorized autobiography

©2012, Wally Metts Jr., Ph.D.

Published by Kadesh Press

Printed in the United States of America

For information about permission to reproduce selections from this book, write to Kadesh Press, 7550 Cochran Rd., Horton, MI 49246 or email wally@thedaysman.com.

ISBN 978-0-9842766-2-2,

Wally Metts is director of graduate studies in communication at Spring Arbor University in Spring Arbor, MI. He and his wife Katie raise barn cats and Christmas trees on a farm south of campus. His grandchildren call him Santa. He blogs on faith and culture at http://thedaysman.com

Forward

I was on sabbatical at the university where I teach, reading several books about Nicholas of Myra, when I received an unexpected manuscript by email which purports to be the autobiography of the world's most widely recognized Christian saint.

All efforts to trace its origin have been unsuccessful, but as a service to those interested in Saint Nicholas I have translated the document from fourth century Greek, using my three years of high school Latin.

Nicholas was, of course, the 4th century bishop whose legend has given us Father Christmas, Kriss Kringle, Sinterklass, Weihnachtsmann, and other manifestations of Santa Claus. Fortunately in this manuscript, Nicholas is able to tell us how he became Santa and how he feels about it.

I recognize that the unauthorized autobiography of a man who has been dead almost 1700 years may be rejected by those who don't believe in him, but those less skeptical will find here a record which I've verified against the most ancient manuscripts; or at least against almost a dozen contemporary books which recount the details of how Nicholas became Santa.

It's a story I have chosen to let him tell himself, with only minor alterations in the historical record and with full recognition of his humble beginnings as a pastor now remembered as wonderworker, gift giver, and both religious and commercial icon.

I hope you enjoy the story as much as I did.

Accepting the gift

They got it wrong, mostly.

I realize nobody wrote it down until 400 years later. And, well, my own diaries and sermons were burned during the persecution under Diocletian. But I'd like to set the record straight, after so many centuries of distortion and exaggeration.

My name is Nicholas, Nicholas of Myra. And this is my story.

I was born in 280 A.D. in Patara. It was a town of some consequence then, or at least we liked to think so. Patara was a trading center in Asia Minor and my parents, Theophanes and Nonna, were wealthy merchants.

They were quite old when I was born. Maybe not as old as Sarah and Abraham in the Bible, but I know my mom did pray for a child a long time. They thought I was a gift. Frankly, they were gracious people who saw everything as a gift.

My parents held their wealth lightly, as lightly as a feather blowing down the stone streets, under the aqueduct and out into the wooded hills. I always knew that everything we had was never really ours.

One of the monks would later write that my parents were "of substantial lineage, holding property enough without superfluity." I guess it felt like superfluity at the time. We certainly lacked nothing.

I had a Greek tutor, for example. He was a bodyguard, actually. I loved to hang out down near the shipyards and listen to the seamen talk about their adventures in Rhoads, Cyprus, Antioch, Alexandria, even Rome. It was more exciting than the market, with all its beads and glass and fabric.

The waterfront was no place for a boy, Mom used to say; especially after I repeated a few words she didn't think I should know. But Dad just told the tutor to keep me out of trouble, more for mom's benefit than mine. There is a lot to learn, Dad said. We both knew trouble is where you learn most of it.

Learning occupied most of my day, actually. And I'm not just talking about school. I was an early reader and a good student and fortunate to have access to scrolls and such. But we also took church very seriously.

In fact, the Apostle Paul had visited our city years

before and we read his letters to the other churches regularly, poring over them and memorizing
them. And we read the Gospels especially. Jesus
seemed so fresh and real to me, even when I was a
kid.

Mom joked that when I was a baby I wouldn't even
nurse on fast days, but I joked back that it was just
because she wouldn't feed me. I was named after
her brother, Nicholas, who was our bishop. The
name means "the people's hero," which took more
than a little getting used to.

Even then there was talk of my becoming a pastor.
"I see a new sun rising and manifesting in himself
a gracious consolation for the afflicted," my uncle
said. I never saw myself as a "new sun," that's for
sure. But I did have a tender heart. I loved to go
with Mom when she went out "distributing to the
necessity of the saints," as she called it. It was often
just a loaf of bread left on someone's doorstep.

From my earliest days I remember our talking,
praying, singing and thinking about Jesus. Because of their wealth, I think, my parents seemed
particularly interested in the Gospel of Luke, since
Jesus said so much there about money. This is
where he says to give our gifts in secret, without
the right hand knowing what the left hand was
doing. It's the only way to do it so God gets the

credit.

In those days the Christians in our city often met in homes, eating together and encouraging each other. My favorite place to meet was at Stephen's house. He and Anna were good friends of my Mom and Dad, members of the merchant's guild and the city council.

I'm not saying I liked to go there because of his three beautiful daughters. I was just a kid after all, if not a precocious one. I just liked that they made everyone feel welcome, even the many slaves who followed Christ—"not as a slave, but as a beloved brother," as Paul wrote to Philemon.

This didn't sit well with every one. Many people were suspicious of us, especially the Romans. The Romans were suspicious of everyone. The empire was in decline and insecurity makes men do stupid things. Even evil things. It was very sobering when we heard that Polycarp had been burned at the stake. And of course we all knew about Nero, who blamed the great fire in Rome on Christians.

But we were a brave and cheerful lot. My uncle Nicholas insisted that a life in service to Christ was a life of sacrifice and joy. My childhood was a lot more of the latter. We were both blessed and grateful.

That was until the winter the plague spread

throughout our entire province, cutting down entire families. Ships would not come into the harbor. Caravans would not enter the city. The moneylenders were cruel and the famine was relentless. Sometimes I prayed all night for the people in our city. I was 13.

And then one weekend both my parents died. Mercifully their passing was short. My grief was not. I missed Mom's laughter, reverberating down the halls. And I missed Dad's wisdom. He always knew what to do. And I didn't.

I still answered the door and tried to help the people asking for help. That's what they would have done. But when the door closed, the stonewalls seemed harder and colder. Like my heart.

But it wasn't time that healed my grief. It was action. I moved in with my uncle and became more involved in his work. I spent a lot of time with the orphans. I knew what they were feeling. And I was learning that being busy was better than feeling sorry for your self. Everywhere we turned there were sorrows enough.

Stephen even lost his fortune when two ships he had staked never returned. He had already lost Anna in the plague. As his debtors crowded in, threatening even to take his daughters, I knew what I had to do. My parents left me a lot of money.

Since I was planning to continue my studies and enter the ministry, it wasn't going to do me much good. Neither were the girls, for that matter.

So, well, I gave them gold for their dowries. Three bags, actually. One for each daughter. I tried really hard to do it in secret, dropping them through the window at night. I don't know anything about the one bag falling in a shoe or stocking or anything like that. It doesn't matter, really.

I just know that Stephen caught me one night, as I tried to sneak down the street behind their house. He was so grateful it was embarrassing. The chronicles got that mostly right. He said: "If the Lord great in mercy had not raised me up through thy generosity, then I, an unfortunate father, already long ago would be lost together with my daughters in the fire of Sodom."

Or he said something very like it. Stephen always had a flair for the dramatic. I'm just glad he got the "Lord great in mercy" part itn there. It explains a lot, as we will see.

I asked him not to tell anyone, but of course he did. I had been giving away a lot of money, actually. There were so many needs. People started to put two and two together and come up with ten or something, giving me a lot more credit than I deserved.

Bankers and pawn-brokers even adopted three gold balls as a symbol of their willingness to help people in need, a reference to the dowries.

People say and do all kinds of things you can't control.

Becoming an example

Regardless of what they say, I did not break my nose in a fight down at the shipyards. Yes, I loved ships and sailors and such, and I spent a lot of time with them. But you have to expect that when you're the bishop in a busy port city like Myra.

And yes, I was a bit of a scrapper, as we shall see. But before we get to the story about my nose, which is not nearly as exciting as you might think, I should tell you how I got to Myra in the first place.

I actually filled in for my uncle in Patara when he took a pilgrimage to the Holy Land. But the leap from student to servant is a big one. I had been leading prayers and reading Scripture for some time. But suddenly people's needs were greater than I ever realized. A loaf of bread was not going to be enough. The answers I had did not always fit the questions they asked.

I tried very hard not to be full of myself. What people seemed to need most of all was time.

Polycarp said pastors were "to be compassion-
ate and merciful to all, bringing back those that
wander, visiting all the sick, and not neglecting the
widow, the orphan or the poor." Given the devas-
tation of the plague, there was a lot to do.

But when my uncle returned, I guess the wander-
lust got to me. It wasn't just the call of the ships;
it was the transformation the trip had made in my
uncle. Always a wise man, he seemed filled with
wonder. He had walked where Jesus walked and I
wanted to do it too.

There was the little matter of passage, however. I
had given away the family fortune, so to speak, but
I was amazed at how so many people chipped in
a little for the trip. In fact I was humbled. It seems
like nothing today, but then the little jaunt down
the coast, around Cyprus and along the edge of
Palestine to the Roman port of Caesarea was a
little more daunting. And then there was the camel
ride to Jerusalem.

The Romans still ruled Jerusalem, of course. But
the Christians there were gracious and, well,
creative. Though much of the old city was buried
under Roman construction, they welcomed me,
secretly showing me the room where the Lord's
Supper took place, even the place where Jesus
died and where he lay until the resurrection.

I remember standing outside the chamber of the High Priest and looking down the rough road to Gethsemane, realizing that Jesus himself had walked that road to give his life for me. What a gift that was.

And then, on the way home, there was the storm. People make a lot of this story. The way they tell it I raised a sailor from the dead and also calmed the sea, like Jesus did. It was a lot more like what Paul did, in Acts. I just prayed a lot. Yes, the sea was pretty violent. Like Paul, we didn't see the stars or even the sky for days. "All hope of our being saved was at last abandoned," just the way Paul remembered his own ordeal.

When the sky cleared and we had drifted back to Patara, the sailors thought it was a miracle. I thought it was a miracle too; I just never thought I should get any credit for it. But the sailors talked about it for years. Sailors are like that.

Anyway, I plunged back into helping my uncle, although I was torn. My trip had changed me, and I considered a monastery and a life of contemplation. There was so much I didn't know and I wanted the time to study it. And it seemed a way to deal with my longing for adventure, to bring it under control in a more disciplined, thoughtful way.

But I had my own Damascus moment. As clearly as God spoke to Paul he spoke to me: "Nicholas, here is not the field on which you must bring forth the fruit I expect, but turn back and go into the world and let my name be glorified in you." The chronicles got this exactly right.

So I never turned back. I took my vocation seriously. So did others. When the archbishop in nearby Myra died, a council of pastors asked me to take the job. One of them had a dream that the first person who entered the cathedral to pay his respects would be new archbishop, and it turned out to be me. Considering that some churches at the time selected their pastor with a lottery, I guess it was as good a way as any.

But I certainly did not feel qualified. There was so much responsibility. And so many needs. Someone later wrote of me: "He was kind and affable to all: to orphans he was a father, to the poor a merciful giver, to the weeping a comforter, to the wronged a helper, and to all a great benefactor."

God, I hope it was true. I was just trying to understand and follow Paul's advice to Titus: "be a model of good works, and in your teaching show integrity, dignity and sound speech."

I have to confess it was easier when I was in the abbot, before I went to jail and broke my nose. Or rather before the Roman soldier broke my nose. After the threats and the deprivation, going without food or water for days, that's when the beatings started.

The great darkness under Diocletian had reached Lycia. We saw it coming, of course. The Romans had burned an entire city nearby when the Christians refused to sacrifice to the emperor. His heir, Galerius, was even worse. But many suffered more than I did. There are stories about wild beasts and iron scrappers and human torches. They are all true.

Perhaps we were spared because we had been kind, not only to the slaves but also to the Romans. Or perhaps we were spared because our distance from Rome gave our captors some space for mercy. But I expect we were spared because God knew we needed strength for the challenges to come.

So in Myra we waited in the dungeons, comforting each other, singing and worshipping, depending as always on the mercies of God. There were wounds to tend and prayers to say. We prayed for the children.

And then one day a guard beckoned me down a long dark corridor and out into the light. I had never expected to see it again, although I imagined it every day. I gathered with my people on the public square and listened to the Edict of Milan. Constantine had conquered Rome under the sign of the cross, guaranteeing our freedom and returning our properties.

I still do not give Constantine the credit. Every good gift, as James tells us, comes down from above, from the father of lights.

It was 313 A.D. and I was 33.

Defending the faith

Yes, it is true. I slapped a heretic. I would do it again, too. But when I first got out of jail, Arius was the least of my troubles.

Many of us had been in jail a decade or more. So helping everyone get their properties back was not as easy as just passing a law in Constantinople. Helping everyone get their kids back was even harder, both physically and emotionally. I spent a lot of time arguing with the magistrates. And I spent a lot more time comforting parents whose kids did not remember them.

And the church was growing rapidly. Because of our persecution many people were taking us more seriously. Hard times have unintended results, almost always good for the people of God. Constantine's own conversion also made it a fashionable thing to do. Jesus said we would have to sort the wheat from the chaff. He never said it would be easy.

This was when I first really noticed the children. They were so fresh and uncomplicated. I'd kick the ball around with them out in the streets or sit and teach them old sea shanties or stories from the Bible. I discovered a piece of candy goes a long way toward a smile.

But when the famine came smiles were hard to come by. We saw it coming: the rain stopped, the crops failed, the hunger began. In some ways it was worse than the plague. Dying is somehow easier than wishing that you would.

The worst part is that you feel like you should be able to control it but you can't. We had money. Money was never the issue. Other churches even sent us money, a common practice since the times of the Apostles themselves. But what good is money when there is no bread?

That's when the riots started, down at the docks. The workers were hungry and tempers were short. Ships passing through had food enough, but not to spare. The seamen were full; the dockhands were empty. It seemed like every day there was a crisis to defuse.

The troop ships were especially problematic. The soldiers would come ashore and there was nothing to eat or drink. They were often unruly and ungracious. Once I went to see some Imperial officers, insisting that they control their men better. They agreed to set some tighter rules and even pay for some of the damages.

But while we were talking I got word that three men were about to be executed. I knew they were innocent. In fact, I knew the magistrate had been bribed. So the officers came with me as I rushed to the square, just in time to stop the execution.

OK, it was a little more dramatic than that. I actually grabbed the sword out of the hand of the executioner, just as it was about to come down on the neck of one of my church members. When the magistrate arrived to protest my interference, he saw the officers and thought he had been found out. He confessed, and the officers arrested him. They took him back to Constantinople. There's no telling what they said.

As the famine wore on I tried harder to buy grain from the ships at port. It was a difficult situation. Cargos were carefully measured and the expectations of merchants and investors were very high. I finally convinced three captains to sell us grain, a hundred barrels of barley from each ship. The grain was not enough, really, but it gave the people hope. And seed too, at exactly the right time. I helped unload it myself.

We paid them. In fact, we paid them well. But it

didn't hurt to have a relationship with men who were just seamen when I was a kid. It didn't hurt to have a reputation as a wonderworker, either. I hope I can be forgiven for not correcting all their misconceptions.

There were stories later that when these three ships arrived in Constantinople their holds were still full. I don't know anything about that. Sailors are imaginative and captains are inventive, especially when it comes to a ledger. But I say compassion accounts for a lot. When I walked around the city with the Captains, showing them the empty markets, there were a lot of hungry children on the streets. "Do the right thing." That's all I said.

Then the rains came. The Lord heard the cries of his people. He always has. There was produce in the market and water in the wells. There was bread and candy and smiles. And thanksgiving. There was a lot of that.

But as it turn out the famine was never the greatest danger that we faced. While we were focused on our hunger, the riots elsewhere were about who Jesus was and what he did. Our faith was under attack and there were deep divisions across the empire.

The most divisive idea of all was promoted by Arius of Alexandria. He maintained that Jesus was not God. This made no sense. If Jesus was not God why did it matter if he died? There would be no salvation and no resurrection. So in 325 A.D. I was glad to go to Nicaea when Constantine called over 300 bishops together to settle this question once for all. The council only lasted a month, but debate seemed to drag on forever.

It turned out to be an argument about a single Greek letter. The difference between an "o" and an "i." But the difference between Jesus being of the same substance as God and of a similar substance is immense.

If God didn't give himself, but only gave someone like himself, then he gave us nothing at all. It's the very heart of grace. You haven't given anything until you give yourself.

I was not a theologian. Although I appreciate that the creed that came out of the council has served the church for centuries, I was a practical man with practical concerns—the needs of my people. But as Arius droned on and on and no one said anything at all, I became more and more impatient. The truth was clear and the needs were great. Finally I just got up and slapped him.

Everyone was stunned, but I like to think I got the conversation going. Damaskinos later wrote that I was "prompted by my saintly vigor," but I was just mad. I spent ten years in jail for this truth and I wasn't going to listen to him deny it.

They locked me up, of course. But the council was short and when it was over they let me go home. The rumors are that Jesus or Mary or the angels visited me in my cell and that other bishops dreamed about it. Even that Constantine dreamed about it. They would have to dream about it, because I never said it happened. I never denied it either.

Let us just say it was a nice jail, as jails go. And I really enjoyed the visitors.

Becoming a legend

I died 19 years after Nicaea, on December 6 in 340. They were peaceful and prosperous years and I had the good sense to enjoy them.

The church in Myra flourished and so did its people. When you have more weddings than funerals, that is a good thing. Stephen had died in the persecution but I baptized his grandchildren. Good kids, all of them. Those bags of gold paid off richly.

The saddest day was the day I buried my uncle. He had taught me so much. I was glad he was in heaven, but I missed his wisdom. He had said I would be a consolation for the afflicted. But then he showed me how.

Mine was a legacy of grace. So many good and gracious people came before me and surrounded me. Toward the end, I would sit in the sunshine down by the dock, telling stories to the kids, slipping them a piece of candy or fruit. It's nice to be older and wiser. It's even better to be gracious and kind.

I never envied the death of the martyrs and wasn't afraid at the end. After all, I had slapped a heretic in front of an Emperor. And I wasn't going to jail after all. Heaven welcomed me and I was at peace.

Or so I thought.

Unfortunately your reputation doesn't die when you do, and mine took on a life of its own. I blame it on the sailors.

I know they respected me. All my life I had listened to them, prayed for them, even loaned them money. Apparently they talked about me a lot. And I am not saying they were always sober.

Over time the three men I saved from execution became schoolboys who had been butchered and turned into sausages. You would think I could be everywhere if you believe half of what they say about me: turning up in storms, giving directions, calming the sea, raising the dead.

But men who had asked me for help when I was alive continued to ask me for help after I was dead. And they dreamed about me quite a bit. They even named churches after me in the ports and along the rivers everywhere. Hundreds of them. By the time I had been dead a thousand years there were over 1500 monuments to me in Europe alone.

The Norsemen were especially fond of me for some reason. It might have been all the stories about me saving ships and sailors but I think they really liked the idea of slapping people you do not agree with. They talked about me everywhere they went.

And they went a lot of places. By the time the Norsemen got me back to Lapland I was an arctic shaman who entered through the chimney-hole in the tents and rode magic reindeer through the sky.

They named a cathedral for me in Greenland, the first one in the western hemisphere. But they also came down through Russia, by way of the Dnieper River. The Russians turned out to be some of my biggest fans. The Greeks too. The Eastern Orthodox generally take the stories about me very seriously.

In 1087 descendants of the Norsemen in Italy even stole my bones from the church in Myra and moved them to a cathedral in Bari, trying to save them from the Turks.

I ended up as the patron saint of sailors, bankers, pawnbrokers, mothers, farmers, prisoners, prison guards, brides, children and unmarried women everywhere. Not to mention Greece, Russia and even New York City.

I can not tell you how uncomfortable this makes

me.

Departed saints, as it turns out, have much less influence than you think (none, if you believe the Protestants). Even if I could explain it to you, you would not understand. Heaven is a garden of delights beyond human comprehension.

But more than that, I was just a guy with a red robe and a funny hat. I tried to wear the vestments of my office with dignity, of course. I wanted to be a model of good works, as the Apostle insisted.

But it was not about me.

It was never about me.

Outliving the myth

The Norsemen turned me into a wonder-worker, repeating stories about my praying for sailors at sea, even turning sausages into schoolboys. Clearly they thought more of me than I did. But when they stole my bones, something happened for which I am grateful, even though it took hundreds of years.

When they moved my bones to Italy, my reputation moved west. As the Crusaders shipped in and out of Bari, on their way to and from the Holy Lands, they heard about me and carried my story home.

They were more interested in my care for kids and widows, however, and in Europe I became known as a gift-giver. This was a turn to my liking.

I am not saying that amazing things didn't happen when I prayed. I am saying I did not do them. That is why we pray in the first place, for God's help. He is worthy of all our praise. I am worthy of none of it.

But to be remembered as a generous man who tried to help people who were weak—or just very young—that felt more comfortable. Giving gifts is natural and right. It is to reflect the character of God Himself, however imperfectly we do it.

You see, when I helped Stephen with a dowry for his daughters I finally got over myself. It is not that I was a proud person, although in some ways we all are. It was just that I turned outward, toward others, and it felt so wonderful I wanted to do it again and again.

And it is a nice way to be remembered.

So my reputation spread across Europe, nurtured by the Miracle plays. By the Middle Ages I was Pere Noel in France, riding a donkey and carrying a basket of toys and treats. In northern German I was Weihnachtsmann, the Christmas tree man, trudging through the snow with a tree over my shoulder.

I have even been credited as Befana, the old Italian woman with a broom who leaves gifts behind, but you will need to talk to Gaspar and his friends about that. That's a story about Wise Men, not about me.

I do not even mind Father Christmas in England, though he is more likely to bring rich food than presents. I lived through more than one famine, so I believe hearty food and stout ale should be welcome on a winter night. Throw another log on the fire and relax. It is all grace in the end.

But it was the Dutch who took me the most seriously. And that's funny, since they had me confused with someone else. In the Middle Ages they were ruled by the Spanish, and there was a Spanish bishop who came there every year with his Moorish servant Zwarte Piet, or Black Peter. He would come with gifts for the children and the needy.

Years later the Dutch got him mixed up with me, and called him Sinterklass. Saint Nicholas. I feel bad in a way.

Anyway, the customs of gift-giving spread, and I get at least some of the credit. Aquinas said my habit of giving gifts in secret was important, and Dante said my care of Stephen's daughters was a model of giving.

I have thanked them both.

Soon schoolmasters made December 6 a holiday, which may explain why kids like me so much. Nuns left nuts and fruit on the doorsteps of the poor on St. Nicholas Eve. Kids started leaving their shoes out, to be filled with treats.

I was said to come through the window, which I assure you is more comfortable than a chimney. It was all great fun.

And then I was almost completely forgotten. At least in the west.

It wouldn't have bothered me, of course. These things are in God's hands. But the Reformers put me on their naughty list. All over Europe they were overturning statues and icons. Some really nice windows that told the story of my life were smashed. And feast days were banned. Not just mine.

Saints were never to be worshiped, I know. But it was a little disconcerting.

Across Europe I disappeared from the church, a sad thing by my reckoning. And I reappeared in the home of common folks, who found my memory comforting and told my story to their children, as embellished and as fantastical as it had become.

And this was pretty much the way it was when the Puritans set off for America.

Fortunately, the Dutch settled Manhattan. New Amsterdam it was then. Within two generations it was New York, and the Puritans were running things. Most of the Dutch were Puritans anyway.

But at least some of the Dutch remembered what it was like to wake up on the 6th of December with a shoe full of candy by the window.

You will pardon me for taking the time to include

here a line or two from the law that governed New York at the time, but it's part of my story:

On Saint Nicholas Eve various persons have been standing on the Dam and other places in the town with candy, eatables, and other merchandise [so that the magistrates] to prevent all such disorders and superstitions…have ordered, regulated and opined that on Saint Nicholas Eve…no persons, whoever they may be, are to be allowed….within this town with any candy, eatables and other merchandise….

Now, a Roman solider broke my nose, and my church suffered under Diocletian. It is no great loss to the people of God to go without candy.

But it is no great gain, either. Or at least the Dutch didn't think so. Their Nicholas cookies survived. And so did I. This was to be my legacy, a kind old pastor, remembered with cookies and stories, an example of charity and goodwill.

But John Pintard wouldn't let it rest. He was a decent enough man, and even helped found the American Bible Society. But he was a promoter, when all I wanted was a storyteller.

Promote he did. By the time he was finished, I was the original patron saint of New York City, and the Dutch had come over on a ship with my image carved on the bow. None of this is true.

He said my memory would preserve the "virtuous habits and simple manners of our Dutch ancestors." But it did more than that. In fact, it got out of hand. Before long I was a commercial icon, not a religious one.

The Dutch had bought the whole island for $24 in trinkets and beads, and as the saint of merchants and bankers I guess I should have been OK with the whole thing. But Pintard and his friends just about ruined me.

One of his friends was a storyteller, Washington Irving. Irving helped Pintard promote New York by writing a brief satirical history of the city that referred to me 22 times and was published on my feast day in 1809.

Before Irving was done I was flying over the tree-tops and dropping down chimneys. I heard a lot of tall tales when I was a kid, hanging out around the docks in Myra. Frankly, this was enough to make a sailor blush.

Well, maybe not a sailor. But it makes me blush. Do not get me wrong. I was a bit of a storyteller myself. I can spin a yarn. But as I said, it is time someone set the record straight.

And that is all I am trying to do.

Finding a perspective

I'm not sure exactly when I became Santa.

Pintard and Irving had made me the stuff of bed-time dreams instead of daytime virtues. But there was more to come.

There was Clement Moore, a distinguished scholar and pastor who used to delight his six children with poems for birthdays and special occasions. His Night Before Christmas was harmless enough as a family story.

But a friend sent it to a local newspaper in 1823 and now it has been reprinted more than any other piece of writing in American history. If only Dante had been so blessed.

Then Moore's poem prompted another family man, a political cartoonist named Thomas Nast, to do over 45 illustrations of me. It's Nast who moved me to the North Pole.

At first it wasn't too bad. I looked something like

a bishop, at least. But by the end I looked exactly like Moore had described me, with rosy cheeks and a stomach that shakes when I laugh "like a bowl full of jelly."

Let me be clear. I was never one of those bishops who made themselves fat while their people starved. I would rather give food away than eat it myself and I often did.

I know enough of poverty to take moderation seriously. Generosity is not the work of gluttons. I know that.

And I know this, too. Haddon Sundblom's paintings of me for Coca Cola in the 20th century only made it worse. I became the best-known Christian saint in the world, but not for reasons I cherish.

Maybe I am being too hard on Sundblom. There is a playfulness about his paintings I find appealing. It reminds me a little of my last days, down by the dock, joking with the deckhands and playing with the children, listening to the deep blue waters lap against the dock.

But thank God for the innocence of children.

It is the children themselves who have kept for me a somewhat gracious image of my true self. Yes, many of them are greedy. They have yet to understand grace. But many of them do understand me, despite the antics of their parents.

And they understand gifts too, which we all receive without strings. That's what a gift is, and no kid ever thought of giving Santa more than a cookie.

True generosity cannot be repaid, only received. This is a theological lesson that comes cloaked in mystery, as many do.

Certainly I regret it when children go to sleep trying to figure out how reindeer fly and not contemplating the mystery of the Nativity. But it's not their fault. I blame it on Montgomery Ward and its red-nosed Rudolf.

I blame it on their parents too, who moved my feast to Christmas morning. It's not clear when this happened, but it is clear why. It's a lazy connection between the follower and the One followed. And it's a lazy connection between the True Gift and the ones you buy at the store.

This has been going on a long time. The Reformers turned me into Christkindel, the Christ Child. And their German descendants in America turned me back into Kriss Kringle. What is a 4th century bishop to do in the face of human nature and self-interest? Tell my story, I suppose. Give glory to God as best I can.

Even a child can grasp the basics. A long time ago a pastor, not unlike their own, would visit the sick and take care of children who lost their parents. At that time many people were hungry or sick.

He used his own money to care for people in his church and he even went to jail for doing the right thing. He liked to play and tell stories, though. He liked to pray and ask God for help. And God helped him.

If the kid wants me to fly, that's OK. Lots of things happened in my life that cannot be explained. Lots of things will happen in their lives too, and they may wish they could fly themselves before it is over.

I remember I did. When I was in prison, I never expected to see the light again, although I imagined it every day. Why quibble about reindeer when I often wished I were a bird.

But I wished for more than that.

My uncle once said, "I see a new sun rising and manifesting in himself a gracious consolation for the afflicted."

As I said at the beginning I never saw myself as a new sun.

But I would hope that even today I could reflect a greater Light. At the very least I hope to be remembered as one who gave thoughtful gifts and made meaningful sacrifices.

None of it will be remembered exactly as it happened, of course.

But all of it can be true.

Want to read more?

You can read some essays on how and why my wife and I celebrate St. Nicholas Day on my blog at thedaysman.com. Just search for Nicholas.

And there are lots of ideas and information at my favorite Santa site—saintnicholascenter.org.

Made in the USA
Charleston, SC
29 September 2012